DEADLY
LETTER

DEADLY LETTER

MARY HOFFMAN

With illustrations by
Sophie Burrows

Barrington Stoke

For the children of Coldfall School

First published in 2014 in Great Britain by
Barrington Stoke Ltd
18 Walker Street, Edinburgh, EH3 7LP

www.barringtonstoke.co.uk

This story was first published in a different form in
Ip Dip Sky Blue (Collins, 1990)

Text © 1990 Mary Hoffman
Illustrations © 2014 Sophie Burrows

The moral right of Mary Hoffman and Sophie Burrows to
be identified as the author and illustrator of this work has
been asserted in accordance with the Copyright, Designs
and Patents Act, 1988

A CIP catalogue record for this book is available
from the British Library upon request

ISBN: 978-1-78112-368-3

Printed in China by Leo

Contents

Chapter 1
Who's It? Not You

Prity didn't know which was the worst thing about her first day at Green Park School. There was plenty to choose from.

For a start, there was the cold. That wasn't the school's fault, but they hadn't turned the boiler on yet. "There's no need.

It's such a mild autumn," Prity's teacher Mr Shepherd explained.

Prity shivered. If freezing winds and damp drizzle counted as "mild", how was she going to cope with the winter in this strange country?

Prity hoped the school dinner might warm her up, but she couldn't eat much of it. There were things they called samosas, but they didn't *taste* like samosas. They were very dry, and the dinner lady served them with a dollop of mashed potato and some bright orange beans. Pudding was an even drier sort of biscuit and a strawberry milkshake.

Then there were all the jokes about her name. Grown-ups didn't seem to be able to stop themselves from saying "What a pretty name!" – and then they realised they had

made a pun and went all red. And after
the grown-ups at school did that, there was
no way to avoid kids calling out things like
"Pretty ugly" or "Pretty stupid" after her.

Where Prity came from, her name wasn't at all unusual. No one felt the need to comment on it. Prity thought all the English names like Jake and Brooke sounded much odder, but she kept her thoughts to herself.

Prity knew English from her school in India. In fact, most of her lessons there had been in English. But they spoke a different kind of English here in Tottenham. When the children spoke to a teacher, they didn't say "Sir" or "Miss". When they told a story they began, "There was this man, right?" – and Prity didn't know who the man was supposed to be.

But the worst thing was playtime. Prity stood in the playground in her warm new coat and shivered as she watched all the children who had been friends with each other since nursery school. She wondered how she was ever going to fit in. There were other kids from India and Pakistan at Green Park of course, but most of them had been born in London and talked with Tottenham accents just like the white children. They didn't seem to mind the cold, the food, or the people. They hadn't got off a plane two weeks ago, or left everything they knew behind them.

A group of children was dipping in and out to see who was going to be "it" for a game. Prity stood and watched them. They had been playing for some time and they kept using a word that Prity knew was rude. But this time a teacher was near by, so they used the proper words.

Ip dip sky blue.
Who's it? Not you.
Not because you're dirty,
Not because you're clean,
My mum says you're the fairy queen.

O-U-T spells out

So out you must go.

The person chosen to be "it" this time was Casey Gill. She was one of the four children who sat at Prity's table in class.

"Want to play?" she called out, but Prity shook her head. She wanted to watch first

and work out the rules. But she still hadn't understood them by the time the bell went for afternoon school. She had spent playtime on her own, not playing with anyone.

Chapter 2
Empty

At the end of school, Prity had to collect her little sister Romila from the Infants. By then Prity's head was hurting.

Children were pouring out of the school and down the road and some of them were very big. A Year 6 boy wasn't looking where he was going and as he brushed past Prity

and Romila, he pushed Prity off the pavement. Tears filled her eyes and she had to blink them away.

The boy stopped and turned back. "Sorry, mate," he said. He was a tall, well-built Indian boy with nice eyes and a big grin. He was dressed just like the white Year 6 boys – and he talked like them too.

Prity shook her head. "It doesn't matter," she said.

The boy gave her another friendly smile. "See you, then," he said, and ran off.

The next day, Prity took a packed lunch to school in a plastic bag. She sat at a table with some girls from her class. They all had pink or red lunch boxes with My Little Pony or Hello Kitty on them and matching bottles filled with juice. Prity tried to hide the paratha and pickle that her mother had stuffed into the bag for her when she said she hadn't been able to eat the school dinner.

But Prity had forgotten to bring anything to drink and she was very thirsty. Out in the playground, in the cold again after lunch, Prity plucked up the courage to ask Casey where she could get some water.

"You should have asked the dinner ladies," Casey said. "The water cooler is empty."

Casey must have seen how sad Prity looked. She ran back into school and fetched her plastic bottle.

"There's a bit of squash left in here if you want it," she said.

Prity drank the sweet, sticky orange drink and gave the bottle back to Casey.

"Are you coming to play Deadly Letter with us?" Casey asked.

So Prity tried to join in the game she had watched the day before, but she kept doing something wrong. All the other children shouted at her to stay back when she tried to step forward, and when she stayed back they shouted at her to run.

In the end, Prity dropped out and leaned against the wall till the bell went. As she stood on her own, she thought of her friend Kamini in India and of how it was only three weeks since they had played together in the road outside her family's house in Kanpur.

It had been warm there and the air was sweet. Where she lived, everything had sharp, clear outlines – the school, the markets, the stalls selling street food.

Here, in this British city, everything was grey and misty and confusing. No one was nasty and some people, like Casey and Mr Shepherd, were really nice. But all the same Prity went home every day with her head feeling too full and the rest of her feeling empty.

It didn't help that Prity's dad wasn't there to talk to. He had a job in Coventry and Prity wished they could be there with him instead of staying in her aunty's little house in London.

Chapter 3
Nosher

At the weekend, Aunty Veena got Prity a Moshi Monsters lunch box and a pair of skinny jeans at the market. Prity's mum made her cheese sandwiches with white bread and packed them in cling-film. Prity didn't feel so different during lunchtime in her second week. But she still didn't know how to play Deadly Letter.

Several times she saw the big Year 6 boy who had knocked her off the pavement on her first day. He always smiled at her and waved.

"I didn't know Nosher was a friend of yours," Liam Duffy said. "He's a hard man."

"He's probably her cousin," Shane Roman said. Shane and Liam both sat at Prity's table in class. "All the Pakis in school seem to be related to each other."

Prity didn't know if Shane had meant to say something horrible, but it *was* horrible. Really horrible. She felt her cheeks go hot. "He's not my cousin," she said. "And I come from India, not Pakistan."

"All right, all right, no need to get your knickers in a twist!" said Shane. "Sorry."

Prity soon learned that the children at school often sounded nastier than they meant to be. And Shane was nice to her after that. Prity never heard him use the word "Paki"

again. Sometimes he even warned her about kids whose families didn't like black or Asian people. "They're racists, best to ignore them," he said. Prity noticed that none of the kids tried anything on Shane. He was a head taller than any other Year 4.

At half term, Prity had her hair cut. Her mother sighed and kept the long black plait of hair to take home and wrap in tissue paper. But Prity felt light and free. She could toss her hair now that it was in a shiny bob round her shoulders. She was walking through the market and practising tossing her hair when she bumped into Nosher. He was looking at DVDs on a cut-price stall.

"Hi," he said. "Nice hair!" Then he put out his hand. "I'm Nosher, by the way," he said. "At least that's what everyone calls me."

Prity shook his hand. "I'm Prity," she said, and then cursed her slowness. Why couldn't she think of a different way to say it? But Nosher just smiled.

"Do you know what my real name is?" he asked. "Nosherwan Jassawalla. Imagine being stuck with that mouthful at Green Park!"

It was funny to think that Nosher had made an effort to fit in at school. He behaved as if he owned the place, just like all the Year 6s. But Prity was beginning to see how she might feel the same by the time she was his age.

Chapter 4
The Rules

When they were back at school after half term, Casey asked Prity to her birthday party.

There were lots of children from their class at the party. It was the day before Halloween, and Casey's mum had got in a disco with flashing lights. The children were all supposed to wear orange and black.

Prity danced once with Nosher and once with Liam, but mostly she danced on her own or with other girls. She was wearing orange silk churidars with a black dupatta that

was her mother's. It wasn't disco gear, but everyone said she looked good in it.

The day after, at school, Prity felt like one of the gang. But then she tried to play Deadly Letter again.

Connor Walsh was "it" and he said, "The Deadly Letter is 'I'." But when he called out "I" a few minutes later and Prity tried to step forward, he shouted at her.

"Go back to the beginning, you stupid Paki!" he said, with a snarl in his voice.

Prity stepped back. She felt too numb to move away from the game and too upset about how Connor had spoken to her to go on playing. Then there was a rushing sound like a whirlwind moving across the playground and all of a sudden Nosher was in the middle of

the group. Nosher grabbed Connor under the
arms and lifted him till the younger boy's face
was level with his.

"Who are you calling names?" he hissed.

Connor just shook his head. "Sorry, Nosher," he whispered.

"You all hear that?" Nosher asked. He still held Connor in the air as he looked round the group. "This little creep is very sorry," he said. "And so will the rest of you be if anyone else tries it."

Then Nosher dropped Connor like an empty school bag and walked over to Prity. "Pick you up after school," he said, and it was clear he was telling her, not asking.

The bell rang and Prity had never been so glad to hear it. Her face was burning. On her way into class, Shane whispered, "I never knew you had a minder. Nice one." And in story time, Casey slipped Prity a note. "He's

got dreamy eyes!" the note said. "Lucky you."
But Prity was wondering if there was any way
she could avoid Nosher at the end of school.

But there he was – talking to her sister
Romila in the Junior Library, where the little
kids waited for their bigger brothers and
sisters to take them home. As the three of
them set off together, Romila chattered to

Nosher as if he were an old friend. At last he gave her a stick of bubble-gum, and then he turned to Prity.

"Thank you for what you did," Prity said.

"It's OK."

"Only ... I wish you hadn't."

Nosher stopped and looked at her in amazement.

Prity rushed on. "I mean, I wanted to work out how to fit in for myself and now they're saying I've got a minder or a boyfriend and stuff like that and I'll never be able to make it by myself if you try to rescue me."

There was a pause, then Nosher frowned. "You've got plenty of bottle, I'll say that for you," he said. "But some of these white kids are so ignorant – like that loser Walsh. They think we're all the same, even though you're a Hindu and I'm a Parsee. Kids like Walsh have never been out of Tottenham except to go to Liverpool to see Spurs play away. It's all Paki, Paki, Paki to them!"

Nosher smacked his hand against a lamp post, he was so angry. Romila watched him with big eyes and blew a huge sweet-smelling bubble. As she popped it, Nosher relaxed and swung her up onto his shoulders.

"So you want me to keep out of it?" he said to Prity. But he didn't sound angry any more.

"Yes, please. But there's one thing you can do," she said. "If you know how – tell me how to play Deadly Letter!"

Nosher said it was a long time since he'd played Deadly Letter, but the rest of the way home he explained the rules to Prity. As soon as he said that it was like "Simon Says", Prity understood what she'd been getting wrong.

"You only move if you've got the letter in either of your names, unless it's the deadly letter and then you have to stay still or you'll be sent back to the beginning," Nosher explained.

And so, within a few days, Prity was playing Deadly Letter as well as anyone. She learned lots of other games, too. By the end of term, she couldn't remember why she had hated Green Park so much. Nosher hadn't walked her home again, but she often saw him in the playground or in the market on Saturdays and he still smiled and waved.

Chapter 5
Bottle

At the start of December, Prity got a letter from her friend Kamini. It was full of all the gossip from back home in Kanpur. It made her feel so strange and muddled that she didn't notice her mother also had a letter, with a postmark from Coventry. When the girls got in from school that day, Aunty Veena's eyes were red with tears, but their mother was happy.

"I have something to tell you," their mother said. "We are moving to Coventry. Dad has found us a flat and we can join him in time for Christmas!"

Prity was stunned. "But what about school?" she asked.

"Dad has already seen the head teacher of the nearest primary school and you and Romila can both start there next term," her mother said. "It's all worked out very well. Isn't it wonderful?"

Prity didn't want to upset her mother, who was so excited about all the family being together again. But she felt as if she had a cold, heavy lump inside her, like a rock she wanted to throw at someone. She would have to start all over again – new people, new games, new rules to learn. Prity felt weary at the thought.

"Can I go out for a bit, Amma?" she asked. "I want to go and tell my friend."

Prity guessed that her mother would think she meant Casey, but she would be too busy to check. She was already sorting out clothes, while Aunty Veena followed her round the house and gave her lots of advice to cover up how upset she was that they were leaving.

Prity slipped out into the street and took deep breaths of the icy air. She knew where Nosher lived, even though she had never been inside his house. He came to the door when she knocked. He was surprised to see her, but he asked her in. Mrs Jassawalla made Prity welcome and went to make some tea.

"Come on then, tell," Nosher said when they were on their own. "It must be something important to bring you out again on a night like this."

Prity nodded. The lump in her chest had been getting bigger and now it was hard to force her words out past it. "We're going away – moving to Coventry," she said.

Nosher took her hand and Prity's tears started to flow. He gave her his not very clean hankie and let her cry.

"Take it easy," he said. When all that was left were sobs and sniffles, he smiled at her. "I won't say never mind because I know you and you're going to mind a lot. But you'll make a go of it. You've got the bottle for it."

Then all of a sudden Nosher jumped up, as his mother came in with the tea. "That reminds me! I won't be a minute," he said, and he rushed out of the room. Prity drank the hot sweet tea with cinnamon and cardamom, and she talked to Nosher's mother.

Nosher was soon back, with a paper bag in his hand. "Here," he said. "I was going to give you this at Christmas, but you can have it now, just to remind you that you can make it on your own."

In the bag was a small green glass bottle. It looked really old and Prity guessed Nosher had found it on one of the stalls in the market.

That night, Prity lay in bed feeling shattered. Of course she wanted to see her father again, but she had been so busy with her life at school that she'd stopped missing him so much these last few months. But now she wished his letter had never come, or at least that it hadn't come so soon.

Prity fell asleep and dreamed of a playground full of strangers playing a game called "Connor Says". The rules changed every time she tried to join in.

Chapter 6
A Good Game

The next few weeks sped by. There were all the goodbyes at school and promises to write from Casey and Shane. Prity thought of her letter from Kamini. She had still not sent an answer.

Christmas in their new flat in Coventry was a bit of a shambles, but they did have a pudding and a tree. They hadn't been able to get these things in India, although they had always celebrated Christmas as well as Diwali and Holi.

The new year came in with snow and the girls got fluffy boots and ear-muffs.

Then came the first day of term and Prity walked with Romila to their new school, Canning Street Primary. It was old and made of red brick – just like Green Park – and it had the same stale smell of food in the corridors.

Prity left Romila in the Infants with her new teacher and she went to join the Year 4 juniors.

"We have a new girl today," her teacher Miss Brown said – just as Mr Shepherd had done a term before. "Would you like to stand up and tell us your name and where you come from?"

Prity stood up and curled her fingers round the little glass bottle in her trouser pocket.

In a clear voice she said, "My name is Prity Vajir."

"That's a pretty name," said Miss Brown. Then she stopped and blushed. A few children giggled.

"Yes it is," said Prity. "But you can see it has some disadvantages. And I am from Kanpur in India." She sat down, her heart thudded hard, and the day's lessons went on.

At break time, a tall, red-haired girl came over to Prity.

"Hi! I'm Lauren," she said. "Want to play?"

"Sure," said Prity.

"Do you know any Indian games?" Lauren asked, trying to be friendly.

"Not really," Prity said, with a grin. "But I learned a good English one in Tottenham!"

And soon all the Year 3 and Year 4 kids in Canning Street's playground were playing Deadly Letter.

Our books are tested
for children and young people by
children and young people.

Thanks to everyone who consulted on
a manuscript for their time and effort in
helping us to make our books better
for our readers.

More *4u2read* titles ...

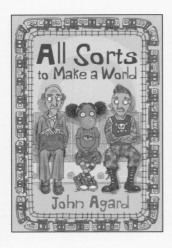

All Sorts to Make a World

JOHN AGARD

Shona's day has been packed with characters. First there was 3.2-million-year-old Lucy in the Natural History Museum, and then Pinstripe Man, Kindle Woman, Doctor Bananas and the iPod Twins.

Now Shona and her dad are on a Tube train that's stuck in a tunnel and everyone around them is going ... bananas!

Nadine Dreams of Home

BERNARD ASHLEY

Nadine finds Britain real scary. Not scary like soldiers, or burning buildings, or the sound of guns. But scary in other ways. If only her father were here with Nadine, her mother and her little brother. They have no idea if they will ever see Nadine's father again.

But then Nadine finds a special picture, and dreams a special dream ...

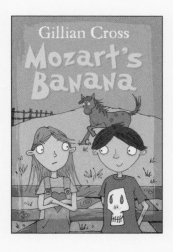

Mozart's Banana
GILLIAN CROSS

Mozart's Banana — a crazy name for a crazy horse. No one can tame Mozart's Banana. Even Sammy Foster failed, and he reckons he's the boss of the school. But then Alice Brett turns up. Alice is as cool as a choc-ice, and she isn't going to let anyone get the better of her, horse or boy ...

Gnomes, Gnomes, Gnomes
ANNE FINE

Sam's a bit obsessed. Any time he gets his hands on some clay, he makes gnomes. Dozens of them live out in the shed. But when Sam's mum needs that space, she says the gnomes will have to go. And so Sam plans a send-off for his little clay friends — a send-off that turns into a night the family will never forget!

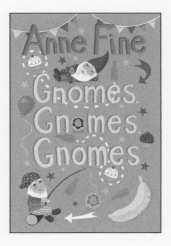

www.barringtonstoke.co.uk

More *Barrington Stoke* titles ...

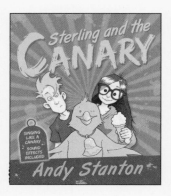

Sterling and the Canary
ANDY STANTON

Lizzie Harris has hair the colour of magic and arms as wonderful as rainbows.

Only thing is, Lizzie Harris won't go out with Sterling Thaxton. Sterling needs help, but who can he ask? Perhaps a canary would do the trick.

Yes, you did read that right. A canary. A very special canary ...

The Story of Matthew Buzzington
ANDY STANTON

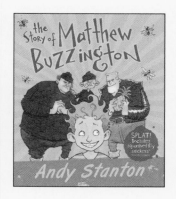

Welcome to the story of Matthew Buzzington. "Who is Matthew Buzzington?" I hear you ask! Well, he's just a normal 10-year-old boy. But Matthew Buzzington can turn into a fly. Imagine that!

It's just, well, he hasn't yet. But with robbers and flying pineapples out to get him, he needs to make his super power work! Can he do it?

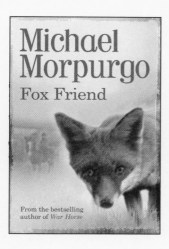

Fox Friend
MICHAEL MORPURGO

When Clare finds a fox cub that has got away from the hunt, she wants to keep him and make him well again. But Clare's dad says foxes are bad. How can Clare keep the cub safe?

The Haunting of Uncle Ron
ANNE FINE

Ian's not keen on Uncle Ron, the world's most boring visitor. Even the voices Uncle Ron hears from the 'Other Side' have nothing interesting to say. Ian can't stand it a moment longer. He must get rid of Uncle Ron. What he needs is a plan – and perhaps a helper ...

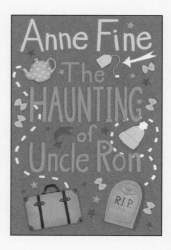

www.barringtonstoke.co.uk